NASCAR BIOGRAPHIES

DANICA PATRICK

KENNY ABDO

Fly!
An Imprint of Abdo Zoom
abdobooks.com

abdobooks.com

Published by Abdo Zoom, a division of ABDO, P.O. Box 398166, Minneapolis, Minnesota 55439.

Printed in the United States of America, North Mankato, Minnesota.
102021
012022

THIS BOOK CONTAINS RECYCLED MATERIALS

Photo Credits: AP Images, Getty Images, iStock, Shutterstock
Production Contributors: Kenny Abdo, Jennie Forsberg, Grace Hansen
Design Contributors: Candice Keimig, Neil Klinepier

Library of Congress Control Number: 2021940196

Publisher's Cataloging-in-Publication Data

Names: Abdo, Kenny, author.
Title: Danica Patrick / by Kenny Abdo
Description: Minneapolis, Minnesota : Abdo Zoom, 2022 | Series: NASCAR biographies | Includes online resources and index.
Identifiers: ISBN 9781098226800 (lib. bdg.) | ISBN 9781644946831 (pbk.) | ISBN 9781098227647 (ebook) | ISBN 9781098228064 (Read-to-Me ebook)
Subjects: LCSH: Patrick, Danica, 1982---Juvenile literature. | Automobile racing drivers--Biography--Juvenile literature. | Stock car drivers--Biography--Juvenile literature. | NASCAR (Association)--Juvenile literature. | Women automobile racing drivers--Biography--Juvenile literature. | Stock car racing--Juvenile literature.
Classification: DDC 796.72092--dc23

TABLE OF CONTENTS

DANICA PATRICK

Taking on the male-dominated sport, Danica Patrick has proven there's room on the pro racetrack for women.

GoDaddy
NASCAR
Sprint
CUP SERIES
GoDaddy
Aspen
Dental
GOODYEAR
TaxACT
GoDaddy

As the first woman to lead the Indy 500 and the first to win the **pole** position at the **Daytona 500**, Patrick has paved the way for female race car drivers.

GoDaddy
GoDaddy
Schuberth
Schuberth
GoDaddy
Troy Lee Designs
GoDaddy
Schuberth
PLATINUM
PLATINUM

EARLY YEARS

Danica Patrick was born in Beloit, Wisconsin, in 1982.

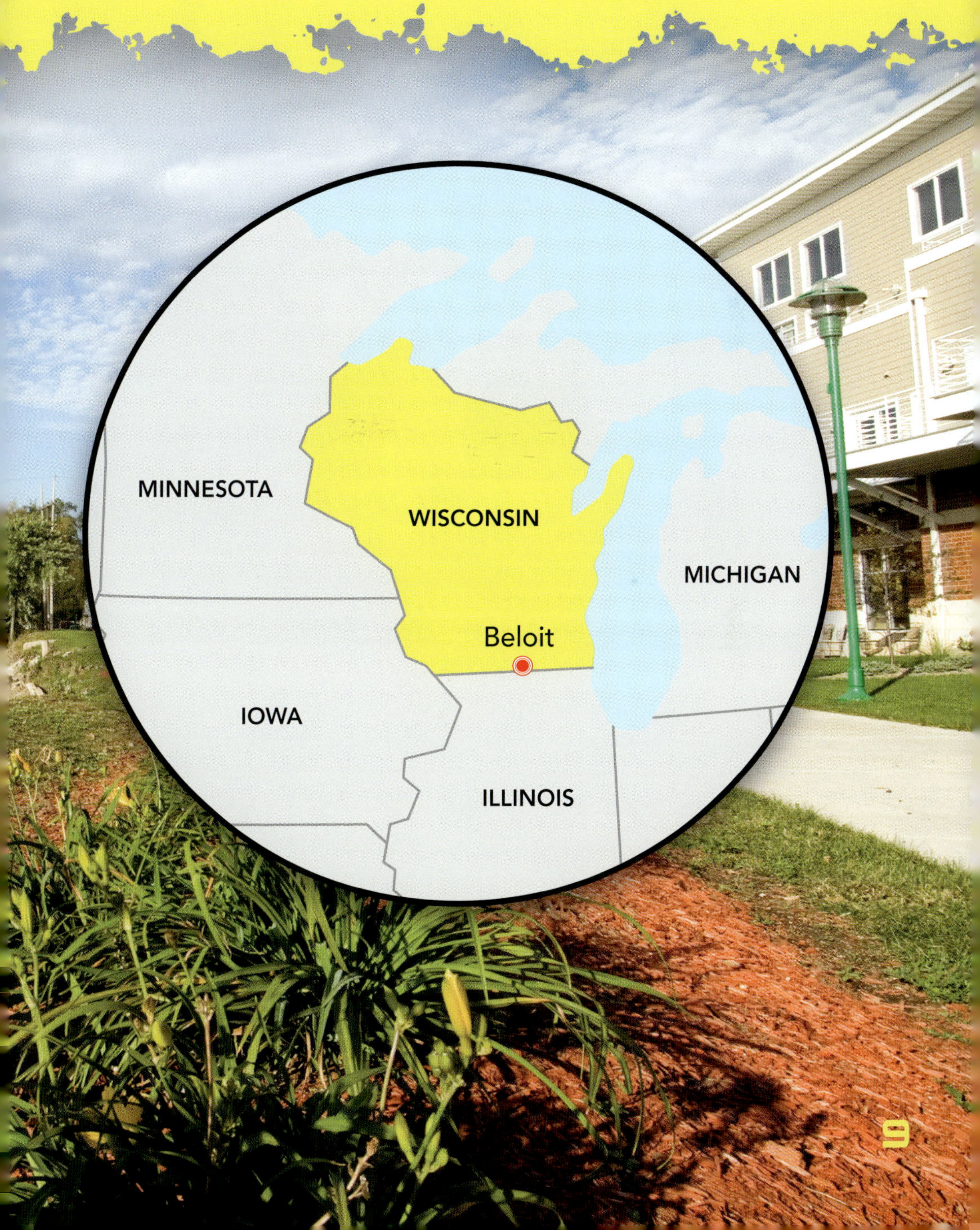

Her need for speed began at age 10 when she would race go-karts with her sister.

Patrick dropped out of high school to pursue racing. She signed with Rahal Letterman Racing in 2002. For the next two years, Patrick finished well, but never won a race.

THE BIG TIME

Patrick's fourth-place finish at the 2005 Indianapolis 500 was the highest for a female driver. She also became the first woman to ever lead the race.

ARGENT
Pioneer
ARGENT
HONDA
bea
sparco
INDYCAR SERIES
ARGENT MORTGAGE
Pioneer
NORWALK FURNITURE
Run-Rite
Danica Patrick

Patrick made history when she became the first woman to win the 2008 IndyCar race. She impressively came in third at the Indianapolis 500 the following year!

Patrick joined the NASCAR Xfinity Series in 2010. She scored a fourth-place finish at Las Vegas Motor Speedway. That was the best by a woman in a national **stock car series**!

Patrick first raced the NASCAR Sprint Cup **circuit** in 2013. She won the **time trials** at the **Daytona 500**! In 2014, she finished in sixth place at the Atlanta Motor Speedway, a career best!

Patrick announced in 2017 that she was retiring from racing. Her last races were in the **Daytona 500** and the Indianapolis 500 in 2018.

LEGACY

Patrick has been the **spokesperson** for many brands. She has been featured in **campaigns** for Coca-Cola, Lyft, and GoDaddy.com!

In 2016, Patrick partnered with the No Kid Hungry **campaign**. She also won the Legend award at the 2018 Kids' Choice Sports awards!

With so many records and wins, Patrick is not just a role model for future female racecar drivers. She is an inspiration for all future athletes.

GLOSSARY

campaign – a series of commercials and advertisements for a certain brand or organization.

circuit – another name for a track that races are held on.

Daytona 500 – the most famous stock car race in the world and one of the races in the Sprint Cup Series.

pole – the fastest time in qualifying.

series – a racing season that consists of several races.

spokesperson – a person who represents and promotes a company or organization.

stock car – a normal car that has been customized for racing.

time trial – when a driver will compete in a race against the clock to secure the fastest time.

ONLINE RESOURCES

Booklinks
NONFICTION NETWORK
FREE! ONLINE NONFICTION RESOURCES

To learn more about Danica Patrick, please visit **abdobooklinks.com** or scan this QR code. These links are routinely monitored and updated to provide the most current information available.

INDEX